Published by Hachette Partworks Ltd.
ISBN: 978-1-908648-53-2
Date of Printing: September 2012
Printed in Malaysia by Tien Wah Press

DISNEY·PIXAR

BRAVE

DISNEY·PIXAR

hachette

Long ago, there was a kingdom called DunBroch nestled in the Scottish Highlands. It was an ancient land, full of stories, magic... and danger.

DunBroch's King Fergus had lost his leg to a demon bear, Mor'du. He had worked hard with his queen, Elinor, to bring peace among the kingdom's warring clans.

The royals had three mischievous triplet boys and an older daughter, Merida.

Queen Elinor regularly gave lessons to Merida on how to become a proper queen.

But Merida much preferred
spending time in the forest
with her beloved horse, Angus.

One day, Elinor announced that three clans would be arriving to compete for Merida's hand in marriage.

"I won't go through with it!" Merida cried.

The queen told her daughter the story of an ancient kingdom, ruled equally by four brothers. When one split from the others, the kingdom went to war, and was ruined.

"Legends are lessons," said Elinor. "They ring with truths." But Merida wouldn't listen – she was determined not to marry.

A few days later, the clans' ships
sailed into DunBroch harbour.
Lords MacGuffin, MacIntosh
and Dingwall presented their sons
to the Royal Family.

Young MacIntosh was athletic, but arrogant.

Young MacGuffin was big and beefy, but his strong accent was impossible to understand!

Wee Dingwall was pint-sized and bewildered.

Elinor outlined the rules of the games, then asked Merida to choose the main challenge.

"I choose archery!" she declared.

That afternoon, Merida watched as the young lords lined up for the archery contest.

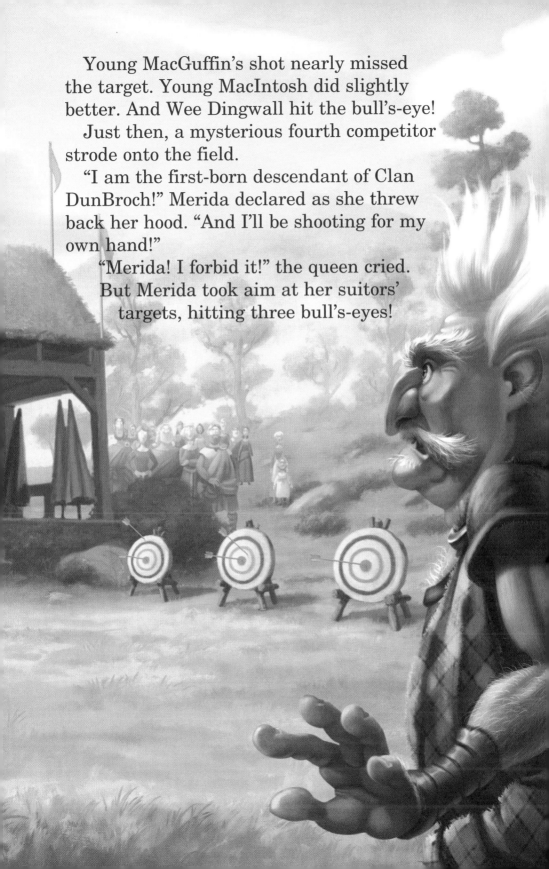

Young MacGuffin's shot nearly missed the target. Young MacIntosh did slightly better. And Wee Dingwall hit the bull's-eye!

Just then, a mysterious fourth competitor strode onto the field.

"I am the first-born descendant of Clan DunBroch!" Merida declared as she threw back her hood. "And I'll be shooting for my own hand!"

"Merida! I forbid it!" the queen cried.

But Merida took aim at her suitors' targets, hitting three bull's-eyes!

"It will be fire and sword if this is not set right," the furious queen told Merida.

"You're a beast!" Merida replied. "I'll never be like you!" Angrily, she slashed the family tapestry between the images of herself and her mother. Speechless, Elinor threw Merida's cherished bow into the fire.

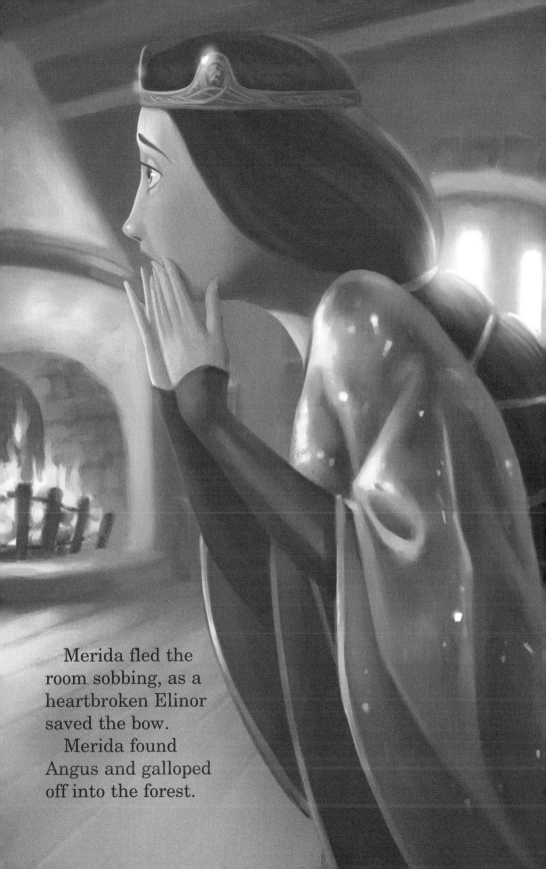

Merida fled the room sobbing, as a heartbroken Elinor saved the bow. Merida found Angus and galloped off into the forest.

After a while, Merida found herself inside a ring of giant stones. She had never seen anything like it.

Mysterious blue lights appeared, forming a trail. Merida followed them to a cottage.

Inside was an old woman selling
wood carvings. Merida could tell she
was a witch.

"I'll buy every carving you've made in
exchange for one spell," said Merida.
The witch told Merida about a prince who had
asked for the strength of ten men. "He was
forever changed," the witch murmured.

"Then that's what I want," Merida declared.
The witch pulled a spell cake from her
cauldron and gave it to Merida.

Back at the castle, Merida offered her mother the cake, hoping it would change her. Elinor took a bite.

As they entered the Great Hall, Elinor stumbled. "My head is spinning like a top," she said. Was the spell starting to work?

They headed upstairs, but the clansmen spotted them and demanded a decision about Merida's husband. Queen Elinor managed to put them off.

Upstairs, Merida helped Elinor into bed. The next thing Merida knew, a huge, furry shape was rising up from the sheets!

"Mum, you're a bear!" Merida cried. "That scaffy witch gave me a gamy spell!"

Downstairs, King Fergus heard a bear roar. Determined to track it down, he led his men through the castle.

With the help of her little brothers, Merida got Elinor out of the castle. "Help yourself to anything you want," Merida told the boys, who loved sweets. But she had forgotten about the spell cake!

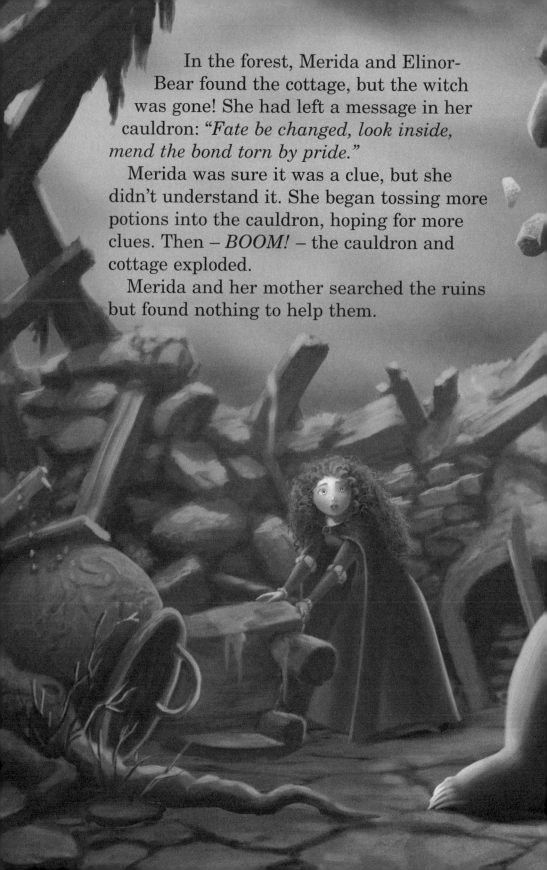

In the forest, Merida and Elinor-Bear found the cottage, but the witch was gone! She had left a message in her cauldron: *"Fate be changed, look inside, mend the bond torn by pride."*

Merida was sure it was a clue, but she didn't understand it. She began tossing more potions into the cauldron, hoping for more clues. Then – *BOOM!* – the cauldron and cottage exploded.

Merida and her mother searched the ruins but found nothing to help them.

The next morning, Merida taught Elinor to fish, so she could satisfy her bear-sized appetite. It was hard for Merida not to giggle. For the first time in ages, she and her mother had fun together.

Then, abruptly, Elinor seemed different. Her eyes turned black and cold – just like a wild bear! Just as quickly, she snapped out of it again, seeming confused.

"You changed," Merida said. "Like you were a bear on the inside, too."

Soon, Merida and Elinor-Bear spotted a trail of blue lights. They followed them to an ancient castle.

Exploring the old throne room, Merida spotted a tablet. It was engraved with pictures of four princes, but the fourth prince had been broken off from the rest. Merida realised it was the prince from her mother's legend!

Then Merida saw claw marks all around the castle. She gasped. The witch's prince had gained the strength of ten men – the strength of a great bear! He was the same prince from her mother's legend, too, and he had become Mor'du. This was his castle.

Then Mor'du appeared. He lunged at Merida, but Elinor-Bear was swift. She rescued Merida, carrying her to safety.

At the Ring of Stones, Merida told her mother, "I know what to do now." She had to get the family tapestry and carry out what the witch had told her to do: *"Mend the bond torn by pride."*

Back home, mother and daughter sneaked into the castle.

Inside, they found Fergus, the lords, and the clansmen fighting – all because of Merida!

Merida was just about to
agree to marry one of the
lords' sons, when, unseen
by the others, her mother
signalled her to stop. Elinor-Bear mimed
what she wanted Merida to say.

"The queen feels… in her heart… that we should
be free to… find love in our own time," Merida
translated.

"A grand idea!" Young MacIntosh exclaimed.

Soon, everyone was happy, their quarrel forgotten.

Merida and Elinor-Bear sneaked to the
tapestry room, but King Fergus found them:
his daughter with a wild bear!
    "Mum, run!" Merida cried.
Elinor-Bear charged
down the hall to
escape.

Fergus locked Merida in the tapestry room, for her own safety. Then he set off to hunt the bear.

Merida was desperate to escape. Then she spotted three bear cubs outside her door. The triplets had eaten the magic cake and they had turned into bears, too!

With the help of her brothers, Merida
escaped from the castle. She and the cubs
climbed onto Angus and raced into the forest
to save their mother. As they rode, Merida
worked on the torn tapestry.

Unfortunately, Fergus and the lords had caught up with Elinor-Bear at the Ring of Stones. They were tying her down when Merida arrived.

"I'll not let you kill my mother!" she cried. And with that, she chopped off Fergus' wooden leg!

Suddenly, another bear stepped into the Ring of Stones. "Mor'du!" gasped Merida. The men ran towards the giant bear, but Mor'du swatted them away. Then he headed for Merida.

With a deafening roar, Elinor-Bear broke free and charged at Mor'du, shoving him away from Merida. After a ferocious battle, Elinor-Bear was still standing... but Mor'du was crushed by one of the huge stones.

Within moments, the ancient prince's soul became a blue light and flew away.

Merida and Elinor-Bear turned to the tapestry. Merida had mended what was torn, so why hadn't her mother changed back?

"I don't care what you are," Merida said, hugging Elinor-Bear. They loved each other.

And with dawn's first light, Elinor became human again. Their bond was repaired, and the spell had been broken. The triplets, too, were human again, and soon everyone was enjoying a big group hug. Their family was whole again!